For my mother and father —S.G.

Illustrations copyright © 1997 by Sergei
Goloshapov. Translation copyright ©
1997 by North-South Books Inc. All
rights reserved. No part of this book may
be reproduced or utilized in any form or
by any means, electronic or mechanical,
including photocopying, recording, or
any information storage and retrieval
system, without permission in writing
from the publisher.

Published in the United States by
North-South Books Inc., New York.
Published simultaneously in Great
Britain, Canada, Australia, and New
Zealand in 1997 by North-South Books,
an imprint of Nord-Süd Verlag AG,
Gossau Zürich, Switzerland.

Library of Congress Cataloging-in-
Publication Data is available.
A CIP catalogue record for this book is
available from The British Library.

For more information about our books,
and the authors and artists who create
them, visit our web site at:
www.northsouth.com

The artwork was prepared with
watercolor, gouache and ink.

ISBN 1-55858-634-2 (trade binding)
TB 10 9 8 7 6 5 4 3 2 1
ISBN 1-55858-635-0 (library binding)
LB 10 9 8 7 6 5 4 3 2 1
Printed in Belgium

Jacob and
Wilhelm Grimm

The Brave
Little Tailor

TRANSLATED BY
Anthea Bell

PICTURES BY
Sergei Goloshapov

North-South Books

NEW YORK · LONDON

A LITTLE TAILOR was sitting on his table by the window one summer morning, feeling very cheerful and sewing busily away. Just then a farmer's wife came down the street crying, "Good jam for sale! Good jam for sale!" The tailor liked the sound of that. He put his little head out of the window and called, "Come up here, my good woman, and I'll buy your wares."

So the farmer's wife climbed three flights of stairs up to the tailor's workshop with her heavy basket, and the tailor made her unpack all her pots of jam. He inspected every one of them, held them up in the air, sniffed them, and at last he said, "It looks like good jam, so you can weigh me out four ounces, my good woman, and I don't mind if you make that a quarter of a pound."

The farmer's wife, who had been hoping for a good customer, gave him what he wanted, but she went away in a very bad temper, muttering crossly to herself.

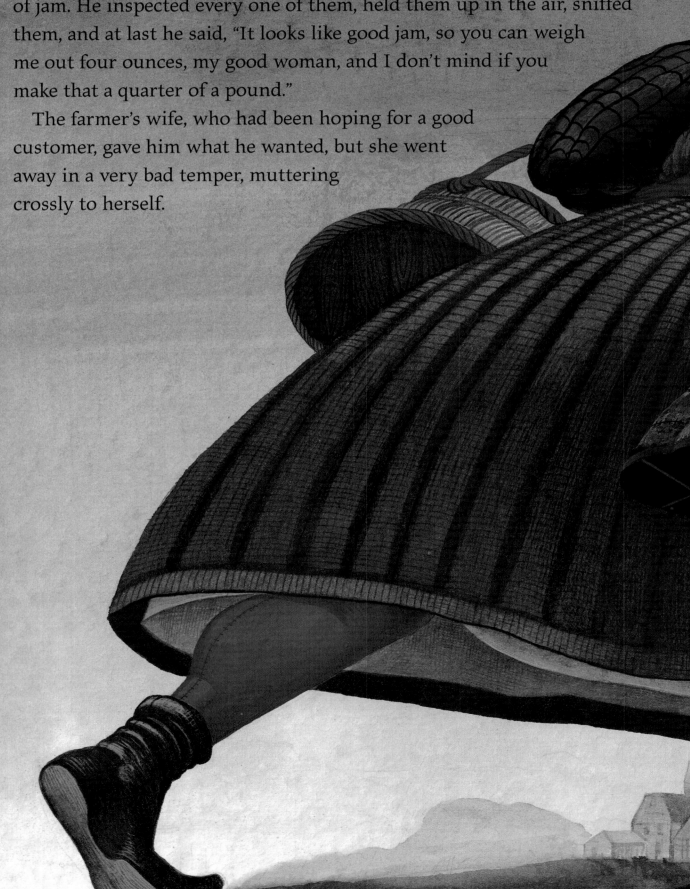

"Well, God bless this jam and give me health and strength!" said the little tailor, fetching a loaf of bread from a closet. He cut a slice right across the loaf and spread it with jam. "This will taste good," he said, "but I'll just finish the jacket I'm making before I eat it." So he put the bread and jam down beside him and went on sewing, making bigger and bigger stitches all the time.

Meanwhile, the smell of the sweet jam rose to the wall, where a great many flies were clustering, and lured them down to settle on the jam.

"Hey there, who asked you to the party?" said the little tailor, shooing his uninvited guests off the bread and jam. But the flies, who didn't understand human language, were not so easily chased away. They kept coming back, more and more of them every time.

At last the little tailor became really angry, and he took a cloth out of a drawer. "Just you wait! I'll show you!" he said, swatting the flies without mercy. When he took the duster away and counted, no less than seven flies were lying there dead with their legs in the air.

"Well, what a fine fellow you are!" he said to himself, amazed by his own courage. "The whole town must hear about this!" And the little tailor quickly cut out and sewed himself a belt with the words "Seven at a blow!" embroidered on it in large letters. "The whole town, did I say?" he went on. "No, the whole world must hear about it!" And his heart jumped for joy like a little lamb wagging its tail.

The tailor put the belt around his waist and decided to go out in the world. After all, he thought, my workshop is too small for such a bold fellow. Before setting out, he looked around for anything useful that he could take with him. He found nothing but an old cheese, so he put that in his pocket. Outside the door he noticed a bird caught in a bush, and he put the bird in his pocket too, along with the cheese.

Then he began striding boldly along the road, and being light and nimble, he didn't tire easily.

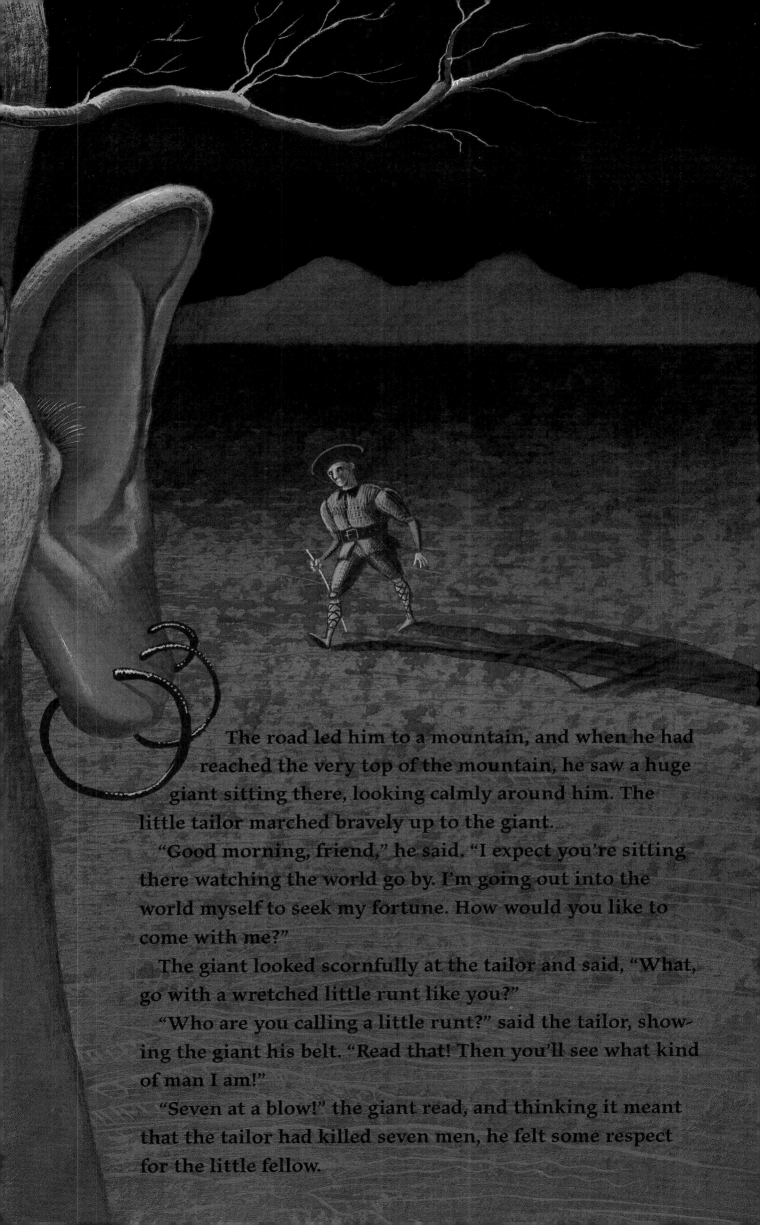

The road led him to a mountain, and when he had reached the very top of the mountain, he saw a huge giant sitting there, looking calmly around him. The little tailor marched bravely up to the giant.

"Good morning, friend," he said. "I expect you're sitting there watching the world go by. I'm going out into the world myself to seek my fortune. How would you like to come with me?"

The giant looked scornfully at the tailor and said, "What, go with a wretched little runt like you?"

"Who are you calling a little runt?" said the tailor, showing the giant his belt. "Read that! Then you'll see what kind of man I am!"

"Seven at a blow!" the giant read, and thinking it meant that the tailor had killed seven men, he felt some respect for the little fellow.

However, he decided to test him, and he picked up a rock and pressed it in his hand so hard that water dripped out.

"Do that too, if you're strong enough," said the giant.

"Is that all?" said the little tailor. "It's child's play to a man like me," and he put his hand in his pocket, took out the soft cheese, and pressed it so that the buttermilk ran out. "There, that was better than you did, wasn't it?" he asked.

The giant didn't know what to say. He couldn't believe the little man was so strong. So he picked up another rock and threw it into the air. It went so high that you could scarcely see it anymore. "Now then, you little dwarf, do that too!"

"Not a bad throw," said the little tailor, "but the rock must have fallen to earth again somewhere. Watch me throw one that never comes down at all!" And he put his hand in his pocket, took out the bird and threw it into the air. The bird, delighted to be free again, soared up, flew away, and never came back.

"How's that for a good trick, my friend?" asked the tailor.

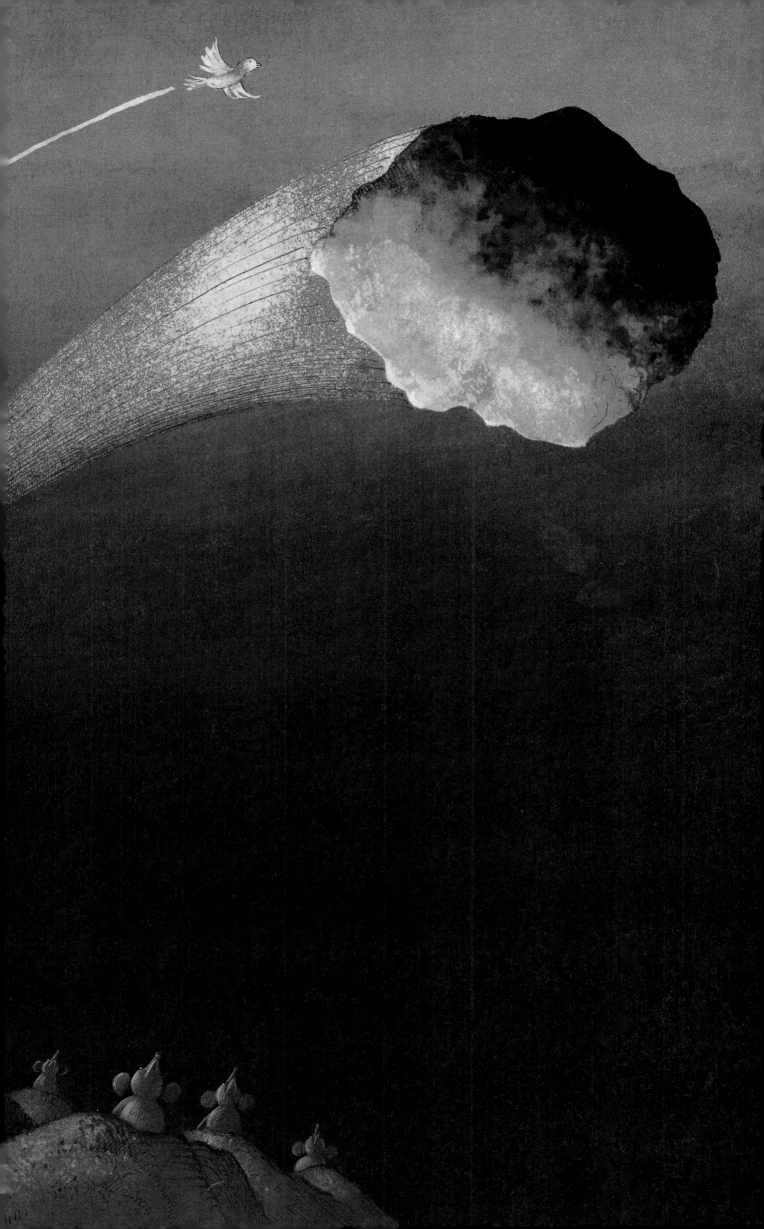

"You can certainly throw well," said the giant, "but now let's see if you can carry a heavy load." He led the little tailor over to a huge oak tree that had fallen to the ground, and said, "If you're strong enough, help me carry this tree out of the forest."

"By all means," said the little man. "You put the trunk on your shoulders and I'll carry the branches and twigs. That's the difficult part of the job."

So the giant put the trunk on his shoulders, but the tailor perched on a branch, and as the giant couldn't look around, he carried the whole tree and

the little tailor as well. The tailor was very comfortable and happy, whis-
tling the tune that goes "Three tailors went riding away through the gate"
as if carrying a tree were child's play.

When the giant had carried his heavy load some way, he couldn't go on,
and called out, "Hey, I'll have to drop this tree!" The tailor nimbly jumped
down, put both his arms around the tree as if he'd been carrying it all the
time, and said to the giant, "What, a great big fellow like you, and you can't
even carry this tree?"

"If you're such a brave fellow," said the giant, "you'd better come home with me and spend the night in our cave."

The little tailor agreed, and followed him. When they reached the cave, he saw more giants sitting by the fire, each of them holding a whole roast sheep and eating it. The little tailor looked around him. Well, there's certainly more room here than at home in my workshop, he thought.

The giant showed him a bed, telling him to lie down and get some rest. However, the bed was too big for the little tailor, so he didn't get into it, but settled down in a corner instead.

When midnight came and the giant thought the little tailor was fast asleep, he got up, took a great iron bar and brought it down hard on the bed, thinking that would be the end of the impudent little fellow.

Early in the morning the giants went out into the forest, without a thought for the little tailor, until all of a sudden he came walking boldly along, happy and carefree. The giants were terrified. They thought he would kill them all, and ran away as fast as they could go.

The little tailor went on, following his nose. When he had been walking for a long time, he came to the courtyard of a royal palace, and since he was feeling tired, he lay down in the grass and went to sleep.

As he lay there, some of the palace servants came along, looked him over, and read the words on his belt, "Seven at a blow!"

"My word," they said, "what can this great soldier want here in the middle of peace? He must be a mighty lord." So they went to tell the king. "Supposing war happens to break out," they said. "Here's an important man who would come in useful! We ought to keep him here at any price!"

The king thought this was good advice, and he sent one of his courtiers to wait for the little tailor to wake up and then offer him a post in the army. The courtier stayed by the sleeping man until he stretched and opened his eyes, and then he delivered his message.

"That's the very reason I came here," said the little tailor. "I am ready to serve the king!" So he was welcomed to court, and given a fine house to live in.

However, the army officers were jealous of the little tailor, and wished him a thousand miles away. "What are we to do?" they said to each other. "If we pick a quarrel with him and he fights us, he'll kill seven at a blow every time. We can never stand up to that." So they came to a decision, went to the king in a company, and asked him to let them leave. "We can never get along with a man who kills seven at a blow," they said.

The king was sad to think of losing so many faithful servants just for one man's sake, and wished he had never set eyes on the little tailor. He would have liked to be rid of him again. But he didn't dare dismiss him, for he was afraid the tailor might kill him and all his followers and seize the throne for himself.

The king thought about it for a long time, and at last he had a plan. He sent a message to the little tailor, saying that since he was such a great hero, he, the king, would make him an offer. There were two giants at large in a forest in his kingdom, devastating the countryside with their robbing, murdering, and fire raising. No one could go near them without putting himself in deadly danger. If the tailor could overcome those two giants and kill them, said the king, he would give him his only daughter's hand in marriage and half the kingdom as her dowry. In addition, he could have a hundred horsemen to go with him and fight the giants.

Not a bad idea for a man like me, thought the little tailor. I don't get

the offer of a beautiful princess and half the kingdom every day of the
week. "Yes, of course," he replied. "I'll soon get the better of those giants,
and I won't need the hundred horsemen to do it—a man who can kill
seven at a blow isn't going to be afraid of just two!"

So the little tailor set off, with the hundred horsemen following him.
When he came to the outskirts of the forest, he told his companions,
"You just wait here. I'll deal with the giants on my own."

Then he went on into the forest, looking to right and to left. After a while he saw both giants. They were lying under a tree asleep, snoring so hard that the branches of the tree swayed up and down. The little tailor, never at a loss, filled both his pockets with pebbles and climbed the tree. When he was up among the branches, he slid along one of them until he was sitting right above the sleeping giants, and he began dropping pebbles on the first giant's chest.

For a while the giant didn't feel a thing, but at last he woke up, poked his friend in the ribs, and complained, "What are you hitting me for?"

"You're dreaming," said the second giant. "I'm not hitting you."

So they lay down to go to sleep again. Then the tailor dropped a pebble on the second giant.

"Here, what's the idea?" said the second giant. "Why are you throwing things at me?"

"I'm not throwing anything at you!" snarled the first giant.

They argued for a while, but as they were tired, they decided to forget it. When they closed their eyes again, the little tailor continued his game. As hard as he could, he flung the biggest pebble he had at the first giant's chest.

"Oh, this is too much!" shouted the first giant. He jumped up like a madman and pushed his friend against the tree so fiercely that the trunk trembled. The second giant paid him back in the same coin, and they fell into such a rage that they started tearing up trees and battering each other with them until at last they both fell down dead.

Now the little tailor jumped down. "What luck they didn't tear up the tree where I was sitting," he said, "or I'd have had to jump to another like a squirrel—but I'm a fast mover, I am!"

He drew his sword and stabbed both giants in the chest a couple of times. Then he went back to the horsemen and said, "The job's done. I've dealt with the pair of them, but it was a hard battle. In their desperation they tore up trees to defend themselves, but that's no use against a man like me—a man who can kill seven at a blow!"

"Aren't you even wounded?" asked the horsemen.

"Not a scratch," said the little tailor. "They never hurt a hair of my head."

The horsemen did not believe his story, and rode into the forest, where they found the giants wallowing in their own blood, with the trees they had torn up lying all around them.

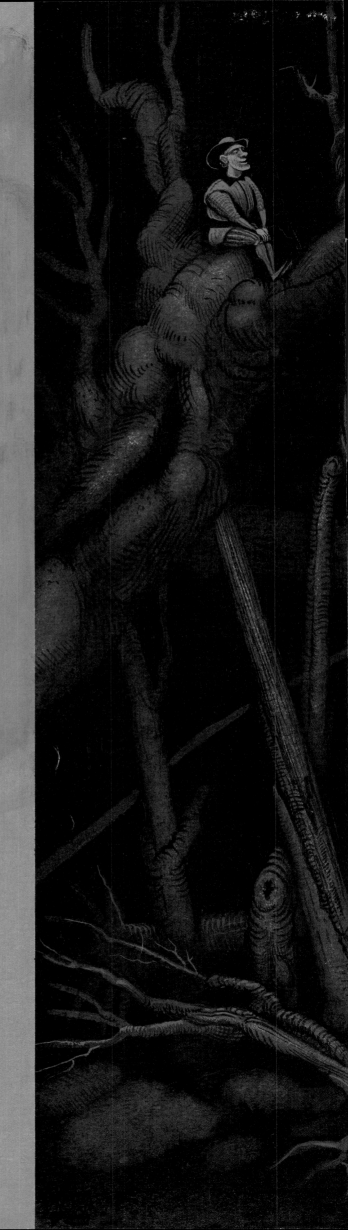

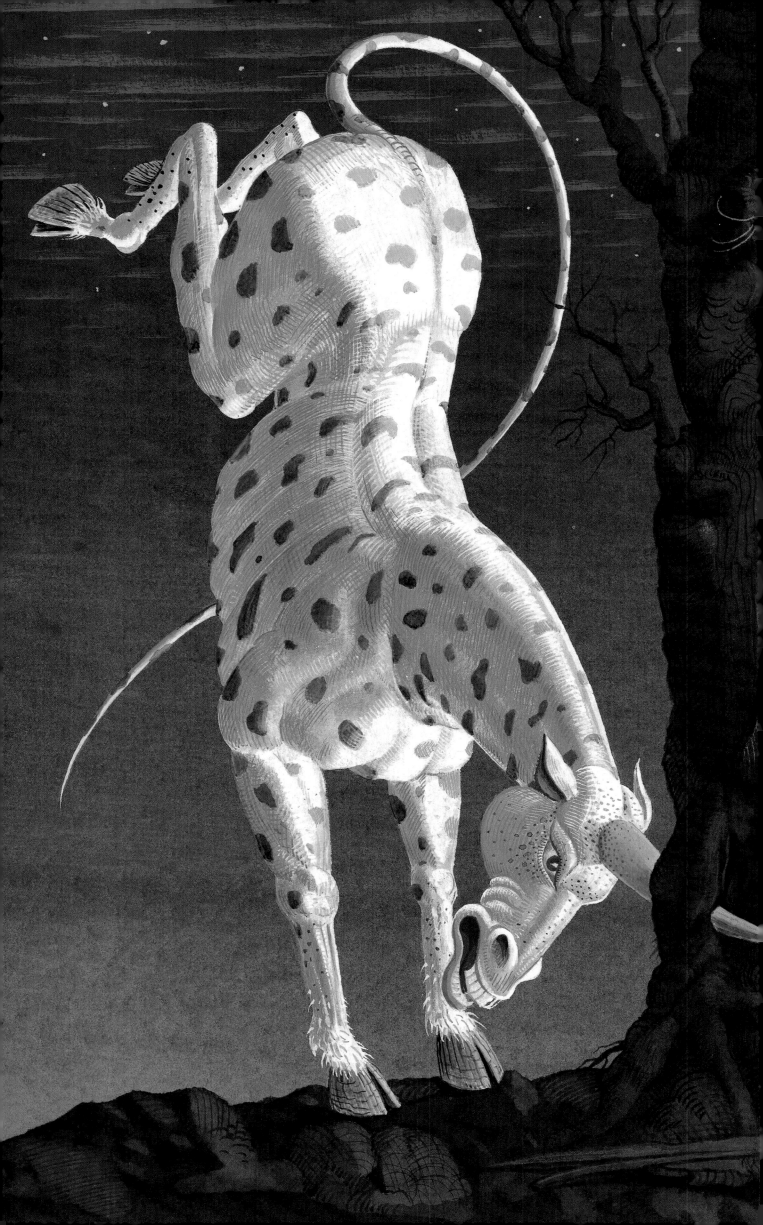

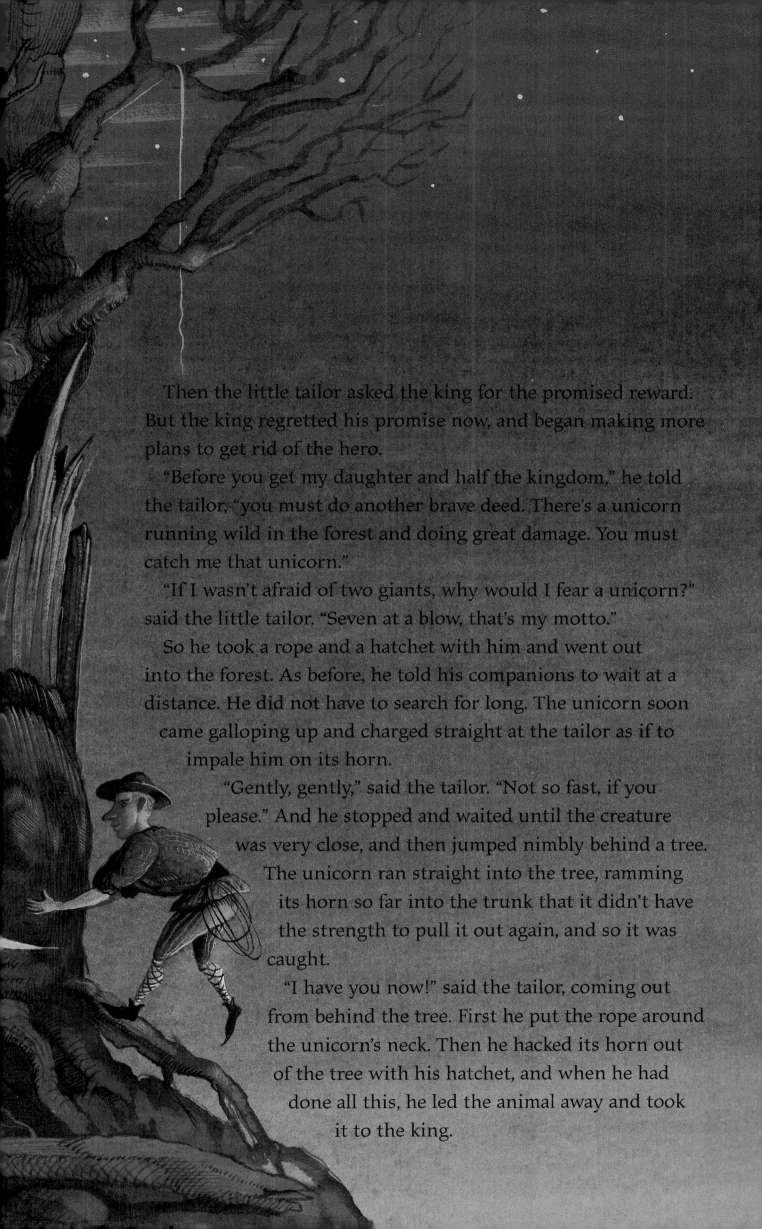

Then the little tailor asked the king for the promised reward. But the king regretted his promise now, and began making more plans to get rid of the hero.

"Before you get my daughter and half the kingdom," he told the tailor, "you must do another brave deed. There's a unicorn running wild in the forest and doing great damage. You must catch me that unicorn."

"If I wasn't afraid of two giants, why would I fear a unicorn?" said the little tailor. "Seven at a blow, that's my motto."

So he took a rope and a hatchet with him and went out into the forest. As before, he told his companions to wait at a distance. He did not have to search for long. The unicorn soon came galloping up and charged straight at the tailor as if to impale him on its horn.

"Gently, gently," said the tailor. "Not so fast, if you please." And he stopped and waited until the creature was very close, and then jumped nimbly behind a tree. The unicorn ran straight into the tree, ramming its horn so far into the trunk that it didn't have the strength to pull it out again, and so it was caught.

"I have you now!" said the tailor, coming out from behind the tree. First he put the rope around the unicorn's neck. Then he hacked its horn out of the tree with his hatchet, and when he had done all this, he led the animal away and took it to the king.

The king was still unwilling to give him the promised reward, and set him a third task. Before the wedding, he said, the tailor must catch the wild boar that was at large in the forest, laying it waste, and he could have the royal huntsmen to help him.

"Easy!" said the tailor. "It'll be child's play to me."

He didn't take the huntsmen into the forest with him, and they were happy enough, for the wild boar had given them such a bad time on several other occasions that they didn't want to go hunting it in the least.

When the boar saw the tailor, it made for him, foaming at the mouth and showing its sharp tusks, and tried to knock him down. However, our nimble hero ran into a nearby chapel, and with one bound he

was out of the upper window again. The wild boar had run in after him. But the tailor shot around outside and slammed the door behind the boar, so the furious animal was trapped. It was much too heavy and clumsy to jump up and out of the window too.

The little tailor called the huntsmen to come and see his captive with their own eyes. As for our hero himself, he went off to the king, who had to keep his promise now and give the tailor his daughter and half the kingdom, whether he liked it or not. If he had only known that it was no mighty warrior but a little tailor standing before him, he would have grieved even more. Well, the wedding was held with great magnificence but little real joy, and so a tailor became a king.

Some time later the young queen heard her husband talking in his sleep in the night. "Boy," he said, "sew me that jacket and mend me those trousers or I'll break my yardstick over your head!"

Then she realized where the young king had come from. The next day she went and complained to her father, and asked him to help her get rid of a husband who was only a humble tailor.

The king comforted her, and said, "Leave your bedroom door open tonight. My servants will wait outside, and once he's gone to sleep they will come in, bind him hand and foot, and put him aboard a ship that will take him out into the wide world."

The tailor's wife was happy to hear that, but the royal shield bearer, who had overheard the whole plot, liked his young master and told him about it.

"I'll soon deal with that," said the little tailor. And that evening he went to bed at the usual time, with his wife. When she thought he had fallen asleep, she rose, opened the door, and lay down in bed again. But the little tailor, who was only pretending to be asleep, began calling out in a loud voice, "Boy, sew me that jacket and mend me those trousers or I'll break my yardstick over your head! I've slain seven at a blow, I've killed two giants, I've captured a unicorn and trapped a wild boar, and do you think I'm afraid of the men standing outside my bedroom door?" When the men heard the tailor say these words, they were terrified. They ran for their lives, and nobody ever dared lay a finger on him again.

SO NOW
THE LITTLE TAILOR WAS A KING,
AND A KING HE REMAINED
FOR THE REST OF
HIS LIFE.